© 1992 The Walt Disney Company

No portion of this book may be reproduced
without the written consent of The Walt Disney Company.

Produced by Kroha Associates, Inc.
Middletown, Connecticut

Illustrated by Yakovetic Productions

Written by M.C. Varley

Printed in the United States of America.

ISBN 1-56326-172-3

A Slippery Deck

Ariel was so excited! While she had been exploring an old sunken ship, she'd found a deck of cards and a book explaining how to play different games with them. She hurried back to the lagoon to show her friends and soon they were all playing a card game.

"Do you have any fours?" Ariel asked Scuttle the seagull when it was her turn.

Scuttle didn't have any fours, so he gleefully shouted, "Go fish!"

Just then, Sebastian dropped his cards. One fell next to Scales's tail, one landed between Scuttle's feet, one even plopped into the water right in front of Ariel. "Oops! Sorry!" the crab apologized, scooping up his cards. "Is it my turn now?"

"It sure is!" said Scuttle. "Go ahead, see if you can beat me!"
"All right," replied Sebastian. "Ariel, do you have any fours?"
Ariel had two fours. She gave them both to Sebastian. "I win this round!" the crab announced, beaming with pride.

They played another game, and then another, and each time Sebastian won. "Sebastian is a good card player, isn't he?" Ariel whispered to Scuttle.

"He sure is," the bird replied. "But it's kind of strange the way he always drops his cards just before he wins."

"I wonder," said Ariel, "if Sebastian is playing fair."

The next game, Ariel watched Sebastian very carefully. Sure enough, just before he won, Sebastian dropped his cards on the ground. "Oops! There I go again!" the crab said with an embarrassed laugh as he moved behind Scales and Scuttle to pick up his cards.

Now Ariel was convinced that
something odd was going on.
"I think Sebastian may be
looking at our cards when
he drops his," she whispered
in Scuttle's ear. "That's why
he wins all the time."

Scuttle couldn't believe
her at first, but the more
he thought about it,
the more he decided
it must be true.

The next day Sebastian asked Flounder the fish and his sister Sandy if they wanted to play cards with him. "Oh, no!" Flounder said, shaking his head. "Not with you! Ariel says you don't play fair!"

Sebastian couldn't believe his ears. Not play fair! Why would Ariel say such an awful thing about him?

All day the tiny crab was so upset, he didn't know what to do. He tried working in his garden, but that didn't make him feel any better. *I thought Ariel was my friend. Why would she think I wasn't playing fair?* he wondered. *It's not my fault I'm good at cards.*

The more he thought about it, the more upset he got. He was so upset that when he saw Ariel that afternoon he hopped up on a rock, looked her right in the eye, and asked, "Why are you telling everyone I don't play fair?"

Ariel was too startled to say anything at first. Finally she blurted out, "Scuttle started it!"

"Me?" squawked Scuttle. "All I said was that it was strange the way he dropped his cards before he won! You're the one who got me thinking he wasn't playing fair. Do you play fair, Sebastian?"

"There, you see?" Sebastian exclaimed. "That's how rumors get started! Everyone believes this terrible story about me!"

"Maybe I did tell Scuttle and Flounder and Sandy that you tricked us at cards," the Little Mermaid replied.

"But isn't it the truth?"

"That's the whole point!" said Sebastian. "It isn't the truth!"

"Then why did you keep dropping your cards all the time?" Ariel asked.

"Because, you see, my claws are so sharp," Sebastian explained, "that if I held the cards too tightly, I would cut them in half — like this. So when I am about to win, I get excited and drop my cards."

"If you knew how to be a good friend," Sebastian continued, speaking very softly, "you would have come to me first, instead of spreading rumors about me." Then he walked off down the beach.

Ariel felt just terrible about what had happened. She told Scuttle she was going to find Flounder and Sandy, and asked him to meet them all back at Scales's cave. When everyone was there she said, "I'm sorry I spread that awful rumor about Sebastian. I hope you all can forgive me."

"Sebastian is the one you really ought to apologize to," Scales said.

"You're right," replied the Little Mermaid. "And I will, but there's something else I have to do first."

Ariel swam to her grotto with Flounder and Sandy following close behind. When she got there she began searching through all her treasures. "What are you looking for?" asked Sandy.

"It's a surprise," Ariel replied, "for Sebastian."

"Sebastian!" the Little Mermaid called out when at last she'd found him. "I'm sorry about what I said. It was wrong of me to spread a rumor like that. I hope you can forgive me. I brought you a present to help make up for all the trouble I caused."

Sebastian carefully opened the box. Inside was a pair of mittens. "Scuttle says these are noggin nuzzlers, and that humans wear them on their heads at night so they can sleep better, but I'm not sure that's right," Ariel explained. "I think you could wear them on your claws instead. That way you wouldn't have to worry about cutting the cards!"

Sebastian loved his new noggin nuzzlers. They made it much easier for him to hold his cards. And he was glad everything was back to normal on the island.

Then one day, as he and his friends were playing "Go Fish," Scuttle dropped his cards.

"It was an accident!" squawked the bird. Then he laughed and added, "You know I'm not tricking anyone — because I never win!"